FANTASTIC MR. FOX

Another exciting tale from the world-renowned storyteller, Roald Dahl

"A fine blend of truth and melodrama...and plenty to prickle the senses."
—The New York Times

"Lively, suspenseful and a whole lot of fun."
—Library Journal

"As lively reading as the author's other two successes, JAMES AND THE GIANT PEACH and CHARLIE AND THE CHOCOLATE FACTORY." *—San Francisco Examiner*

"Roald Dahl has come up with another winner. Small children—and not so small—will love this delightfully witty and exciting tale."
—Children's Book World

FANTASTIC MR. FOX

BY

ROALD DAHL

ILLUSTRATIONS BY DONALD CHAFFIN

A BANTAM SKYLARK BOOK®

TORONTO · NEW YORK · LONDON · SYDNEY · AUCKLAND

*This low-priced Bantam Book
has been completely reset in a type face
designed for easy reading, and was printed
from new plates. It contains the complete
text of the original hard-cover edition.*
NOT ONE WORD HAS BEEN OMITTED.

RL 6, IL age 9 and up

FANTASTIC MR. FOX

*A Bantam Skylark Book / published by arrangement with
Alfred A. Knopf, Inc.*

PRINTING HISTORY

*Knopf edition published October 1970
10 printings through August 1977*

*Bantam Skylark edition / October 1978
12 printings through January 1982*

*Bantam Books are published by Bantam Books, Inc. Its trademark,
consisting of the words "Bantam Books" and the portrayal of a
rooster, is Registered in U.S. Patent and Trademark Office and in
other countries. Marca Registrada. Bantam Books, Inc., 666 Fifth
Avenue, New York, New York 10103.*

PRINTED IN THE UNITED STATES OF AMERICA

CW   16   15   14   13

TO OLIVIA

CONTENTS

FANTASTIC MR. FOX

FARMER BOGGIS   FARMER BUNCE   FARMER BEAN

1

THE THREE FARMERS

Down in the valley there were three farms. The owners of these farms had done well. They were rich men. They were also nasty men. All three of them were about as nasty and mean as any men you could meet. Their names were Farmer Boggis, Farmer Bunce and Farmer Bean.

Boggis was a chicken farmer. He kept thousands of chickens. He was enormously fat. This was because he ate three boiled chickens smothered with dumplings every day for breakfast, lunch and supper.

Bunce was a duck-and-goose farmer. He kept thousands of ducks and geese. He was a kind of pot-bellied dwarf. He was so short his chin would have been under water in the shallow end of any swimming pool in the world. His food was doughnuts and goose livers. He mashed the livers into a disgusting paste and then stuffed the paste into the doughnuts. This diet gave him a tummy ache and a beastly temper.

Bean was a turkey-and-apple farmer. He kept thousands of turkeys in an orchard full of apple trees. He never ate any food at all. Instead, he drank gallons of strong cider which he made from the apples in his orchard. He was as thin as a pencil and the cleverest of them all.

Boggis and Bunce and Bean
One fat, one short, one lean.
These horrible crooks
So different in looks
Were nonetheless equally mean.

That is what the children round about used to sing when they saw them.

2

MR. FOX

On a hill above the valley there were woods.

In the woods there was a huge tree.

Under the tree there was a hole.

In the hole lived Mr. Fox and Mrs. Fox and their four Small Foxes.

Every evening as soon as it got dark, Mr. Fox would say to Mrs. Fox, "Well, my darling, what shall it be this time? A plump chicken from Boggis? A duck or a goose from Bunce? Or a nice turkey from Bean?" And when Mrs. Fox had told him what she wanted, Mr. Fox would creep down into the valley in the darkness of the night and help himself.

Boggis and Bunce and Bean knew very well what was going on, and it made them wild with rage. They were not men who liked to give anything away. Less still did they like anything to be stolen from them. So every night each of them would take his shotgun

and hide in a dark place somewhere on his own farm, hoping to catch the robber.

But Mr. Fox was too clever for them. He always approached a farm with the wind blowing in his face, and this meant that if any man were lurking in the shadows ahead, the wind would carry the smell of that man to Mr. Fox's nose from far away. Thus, if Mr. Boggis were hiding behind his Chicken House Number One, Mr. Fox would smell him out from fifty yards off and quickly change direction, heading for Chicken House Number Four at the other end of the farm.

"Dang and blast that lousy beast!" cried Boggis.

"I'd like to rip his guts out!" said Bunce.

"He must be killed!" cried Bean.

"But how?" said Boggis. "How on earth can we catch the blighter?"

Bean picked his nose delicately with a long finger. "I have a plan," he said.

"You've never had a decent plan yet," said Bunce.

"Shut up and listen," said Bean. "Tomorrow night we will all hide just outside the hole where the fox lives. We will wait there until he comes out. Then . . . *Bang! Bang-bang-bang.*"

"Very clever," said Bunce. "But first we shall have to find the hole."

"My dear Bunce, I've already found it," said the crafty Bean. "It's up in the woods on the hill. It's under a huge tree . . . "

3

THE SHOOTING

"Well, my darling," said Mr. Fox. "What shall it be tonight?"

"I think we'll have duck tonight," said Mrs. Fox.

"Bring us two fat ducks, if you please. One for you and me, and one for the children."

"Ducks it shall be!" said Mr. Fox. "Bunce's best!"

"Now do be careful," said Mrs. Fox.

"My darling," said Mr. Fox, "I can smell those goons a mile away. I can even smell one from the other. Boggis gives off a filthy stink of rotten chicken skins. Bunce reeks of goose livers, and as for Bean, the fumes of apple cider hang around him like poisonous gases."

"Yes, but just don't get careless," said Mrs. Fox. "You know they'll be waiting for you, all three of them."

"Don't you worry about me," said Mr. Fox. "I'll see you later."

But Mr. Fox would not have been quite so cocky had he known exactly *where* the three farmers were waiting at that moment. They were just outside the entrance to the hole, each one crouching behind a tree with his gun loaded. And what is more, they had chosen their positions very carefully, making sure that the wind was not blowing from them towards the fox's hole. In fact, it was blowing in the opposite direction. There was no chance of them being "smelled out."

Mr. Fox crept up the dark tunnel to the

mouth of his hole. He poked his long hand-some face out into the night air and sniffed once.

He moved an inch or two forward and stopped.

He sniffed again. He was always especially careful when coming out from his hole.

He inched forward a little more. The front half of his body was now in the open.

His black nose twitched from side to side, sniffing and sniffing for the scent of danger. He found none, and he was just about to go trotting forward into the woods when he heard or thought he heard a tiny noise, a soft rustling sound, as though someone had moved a foot ever so gently through a patch of dry leaves.

Mr. Fox flattened his body against the ground and lay very still, his ears pricked. He waited a long time, but he heard nothing more.

"It must have been a field mouse," he told himself, "or some other small animal."

He crept a little further out of the hole . . . then further still. He was almost right out in the open now. He took a last careful look around. The woods were murky and very still. Somewhere in the sky the moon was shining.

Just then, his sharp night-eyes caught a glint of something bright behind a tree not far away. It was a small silver speck of moonlight shining on a polished surface. Mr. Fox lay still, watching it. What on earth was it? Now it was moving. It was coming up and up . . . *Great heavens! It was the barrel of a gun!* Quick as a whip, Mr. Fox jumped back into his hole and at that same instant the entire woods seemed to explode around him. *Bang-bang! Bang-bang! Bang-bang!*

The smoke from the three guns floated upward in the night air. Boggis and Bunce and Bean came out from behind their trees and walked toward the hole.

"Did we get him?" said Bean.

One of them shone a flashlight on the hole, and there on the ground, in the circle of light, half in and half out of the hole, lay the poor tattered blood-stained remains of . . . a fox's tail. Bean picked it up. "We got the tail but we missed the fox," he said, tossing the thing away.

"Dang and blast!" said Boggis. "We shot too

late. We should have let fly the moment he poked his head out."

"He won't be poking it out again in a hurry," Bunce said.

Bean pulled a flask from his pocket and took a swig of cider. Then he said, "It'll take three days at least before he gets hungry

enough to come out again. I'm not sitting around here waiting for that. Let's dig him out."

"Ah," said Boggis. "Now you're talking sense. We can dig him out in a couple of hours. We know he's there."

"I reckon there's a whole family of them down that hole," Bunce said.

"Then we'll have the lot," said Bean. "Get the shovels!"

4

THE TERRIBLE SHOVELS

Down in the hole, Mrs. Fox was tenderly licking the stump of Mr. Fox's tail to stop the bleeding. "It was the finest tail for miles around," she said between licks.

"It hurts," said Mr. Fox.

"I know it does, sweetheart. But it'll soon get better."

"And it will soon grow again, Dad," said one of the Small Foxes.

"It will never grow again," said Mr. Fox. "I shall be tail-less for the rest of my life." He looked very glum.

There was no food for the foxes that night, and soon the children dozed off. Then Mrs. Fox dozed off. But Mr. Fox couldn't sleep because of the pain in the stump of his tail. "Well," he thought, "I suppose I'm lucky to be alive at all. And now they've found our hole, we're going to have to move out as soon as

possible. We'll never get any peace if we . . .
What was *that?*" He turned his head sharply
and listened. The noise he heard now was the
most frightening noise a fox can ever hear—
the scrape-scrape-scraping of shovels digging
into the soil.

"Wake up!" he shouted. "They're digging
us out!"

Mrs. Fox was wide awake in one second.

She sat up, quivering all over. "Are you sure that's it?" she whispered.

"I'm positive! Listen!"

"They'll kill my children!" cried Mrs. Fox.

"Never!" said Mr. Fox.

"But darling, they will!" sobbed Mrs. Fox. "You know they will!"

Scrunch, scrunch, scrunch went the shovels above their heads. Small stones and bits of earth began falling from the roof of the tunnel.

"How will they kill us, Mummy?" asked one of the Small Foxes. His round black eyes were huge with fright. "Will there be dogs?" he said.

Mrs. Fox began to cry. She gathered her four children close to her and held them tight.

Suddenly there was an especially loud crunch above their heads and the sharp end of a shovel came right through the ceiling. The sight of this awful thing seemed to have an electric effect upon Mr. Fox. He jumped up and shouted, "I've got it! Come on! There's not a moment to lose! Why didn't I think of it before!"

"Think of what, Dad?"

"A fox can dig quicker than a man!" shouted Mr. Fox, beginning to dig. "Nobody in the world can dig as quick as a fox!"

The soil began to fly out furiously behind Mr. Fox as he started to dig for dear life with his front feet. Mrs. Fox ran forward to help him. So did the four children.

"Go downward!" ordered Mr. Fox. "We've got to go deep! As deep as we possibly can!"

The tunnel began to grow longer and longer. It sloped steeply downward. Deeper and deeper below the surface of the ground it went. The mother and the father and all four of the children were digging together. Their front legs were moving so fast you couldn't see them. And gradually the scrunching and scraping of the shovels became fainter and fainter.

After about an hour, Mr. Fox stopped digging. "Hold it!" he said. They all stopped. They turned and looked back up the long tunnel they had just dug. All was quiet. "Phew!" said Mr. Fox. "I think we've done it! They'll never get as deep as this. Well done everyone!"

They all sat down, panting for breath. And Mrs. Fox said to her children, "I should like you to know that if it weren't for your father we would all be dead by now. Your father is a fantastic fox."

Mr. Fox looked at his wife and he smiled. He loved her more than ever when she said things like that.

5

THE TERRIBLE TRACTORS

As the sun rose the next morning, Boggis and
Bunce and Bean were still digging. They had
dug a hole so deep you could have put a house
into it. But they had not yet come to the end of
the fox's tunnel. They were all very tired and
cross.

"Dang and blast!" said Boggis. "Whose rotten idea was this?"

"Bean's idea," said Bunce.

Boggis and Bunce both stared at Bean.
Bean took another swig of cider, then put the
flask back into his pocket without offering it
to the others. "Listen," he said angrily, "I
want that fox! I'm going to get that fox! I'm
not giving in till I've strung him up over my
front porch dead as a dumpling!"

"We can't get him by digging, that's for
sure," said the fat Boggis. "I've had enough of
digging."

Bunce, the little pot-bellied dwarf, looked up at Bean and said, "Have you got any more stupid ideas, then?"

"What?" said Bean. "I can't hear you." Bean never took a bath. He never even washed. As a result, his ear holes were clogged with all kinds of muck and wax and bits of chewing gum and dead flies and stuff like that. This made him deaf. "Speak louder," he said to Bunce, and Bunce shouted back, "Got any more stupid ideas?"

Bean rubbed the back of his neck with a dirty finger. He had a boil coming there and it itched. "What we need on this job," he said, "is machines . . . *mechanical* shovels. We'll have him out in five minutes with *mechanical* shovels."

This was a pretty good idea and the other two had to admit it.

"All right then," Bean said, taking charge. "Boggis, you stay here and see that the fox doesn't escape. Bunce and I will go and fetch our machinery. If he tries to get out, shoot him quick."

The long, thin Bean walked away. The tiny Bunce trotted after him. The fat Boggis stayed where he was with his gun pointing at the fox hole.

Soon, two enormous caterpillar tractors with mechanical shovels on their front ends came clanking into the wood. Bean was driving one, Bunce the other. The machines were both black. They were murderous, brutal-looking monsters.

"Here we go, then!" shouted Bean.

"Death to the fox!" shouted Bunce.

The machines went to work, biting huge mouthfuls of soil out of the hill. The big tree under which Mr. Fox had dug his hole in the first place was toppled like a matchstick. On all sides, rocks were sent flying and trees were falling and the noise was deafening.

Down in the tunnel the foxes crouched, listening to the terrible clanging and banging overhead.

"What's happening, Dad?" cried the Small Foxes. "What are they doing?"

Mr. Fox didn't know what was happening or what they were doing.

"It's an earthquake!" cried Mrs. Fox.

"Look!" said one of the Small Foxes. "Our tunnel's gotten shorter! I can see daylight!"

They all looked round, and yes, the mouth of the tunnel was only a few feet away from them now, and in the circle of daylight be-

yond they could see the two huge black tractors almost on top of them.

"Tractors!" shouted Mr. Fox. "And *me-chanical* shovels! Dig for your lives! *Dig, dig, dig!*"

6

THE RACE

Now there began a desperate race, the machines against the foxes. In the beginning, the hill looked like this:

After about an hour, as the machines bit away more and more soil from the hilltop, it looked like this:

Sometimes the foxes would gain a little ground and the clanking noises would grow fainter and Mr. Fox would say, "We're going to make it! I'm sure we are!" But then a few moments later, the machines would come back at them and the crunch of the mighty shovels would get louder and louder. Once the foxes actually saw the sharp metal edge of one of the shovels as it scraped up the earth just behind them.

"Keep going, my darlings!" panted Mr. Fox. "Don't give up!"

"Keep going!" the fat Boggis shouted to Bunce and Bean. "We'll get him any moment now!"

"Have you caught sight of him yet?" Bean called back.

"Not yet," shouted Boggis. "But I think you're close!"

"I'll pick him up with my bucket!" shouted Bunce. "I'll chop him to pieces!"

But by lunchtime the machines were still at it. And so were the poor foxes. The hill now looked like this:

The farmers didn't stop for lunch; they were too keen to finish the job.

"Hey there, Mr. Fox!" yelled Bunce, leaning out of his tractor. "We're coming to get you now!"

"You've had your last chicken!" yelled Boggis. "You'll never come prowling around *my* farm again!"

A sort of madness had taken hold of the three men. The tall skinny Bean and dwarfish pot-bellied Bunce were driving their machines like maniacs, racing the motors and making the shovels dig at a terrific speed. The fat Boggis was hopping about like a dervish and shouting, "Faster! Faster!"

By five o'clock in the afternoon this is what had happened to the hill:

The hole the machines had dug was like the crater of a volcano. It was such an extraordinary sight that crowds of people came rushing out from the surrounding villages to have a look. They stood on the edge of the crater and stared down at Boggis and Bunce and Bean.

"Hey there, Boggis! What's going on?"

"We're after a fox!"

"You must be mad!"

The people jeered and laughed. But this only made the three farmers more furious and more obstinate and more determined than ever not to give up until they had caught the fox.

1

"WE'LL NEVER LET HIM GO"

At six o'clock in the evening, Bean switched off the motor of his tractor and climbed down from the driver's seat. Bunce did the same. Both men had had enough. They were tired and stiff from driving the tractors all day. They were also hungry. Slowly they walked over to the small fox's hole in the bottom of the huge crater. Bean's face was purple with rage. Bunce was cursing the fox with dirty words that cannot be printed. Boggis came waddling up. "Dang and blast that filthy stinking fox!" he said. "What the heck do we do now?"

"I'll tell you what we *don't* do," Bean said. "We don't let him go!"

"We'll never let him go!" Bunce declared.

"Never never never!" cried Boggis.

"Did you hear that, Mr. Fox!" yelled Bean, bending low and shouting down the hole.

"It's not over yet, Mr. Fox! We're not going home till we've strung you up dead as a dingbat!" Whereupon the three men all shook hands with one another and swore a solemn oath that they would not go back to their farms until the fox was caught.

"What's the next move?" asked Bunce, the pot-bellied dwarf.

"We're sending you down the hole to fetch him up," said Bean. "Down you go, you miserable midget!"

"Not me!" screamed Bunce, running away.

Bean made a sickly smile. When he smiled you saw his scarlet gums. You saw more gums than teeth. "Then there's only one thing to do," he said. "We starve him out. We camp here day and night watching the hole. He'll come out in the end. He'll have to."

So Boggis and Bunce and Bean sent messages down to their farms asking for tents, sleeping bags and supper.

8

THE FOXES BEGIN TO STARVE

That evening three tents were put up in the crater on the hill—one for Boggis, one for Bunce and one for Bean. The tents surrounded Mr. Fox's hole. And the three farmers sat outside their tents eating their supper. Boggis had three boiled chickens smothered in dumplings, Bunce had six doughnuts filled with disgusting goose-liver paste, and Bean had two gallons of cider. All three of them kept their guns beside them.

Boggis picked up a steaming chicken and held it close to the fox's hole. "Can you smell this, Mr. Fox?" he shouted. "Lovely tender chicken! Why don't you come up and get it?"

The rich scent of chicken wafted down the tunnel to where the foxes were crouching.

"Oh Dad," said one of the Small Foxes, "couldn't we just sneak up and snatch it out of his hand?"

"Don't you dare!" said Mrs. Fox. "That's just what they want you to do."

"But we're so *hungry!*" they cried. "How long will it be till we get something to eat?"

Their mother didn't answer them. Nor did their father. There was no answer to give.

As darkness fell, Bunce and Bean switched on the powerful headlights of the two tractors and shone them onto the hole. "Now," said Bean, "we'll take it in turn to keep watch. One watches while two sleep, and so on all through the night."

Boggis said, "What if the fox digs a hole right through the hill and comes out on the other side? You didn't think of that one, did you?"

"Of course I did," said Bean, pretending he had.

"Go on, then, tell us the answer," said Boggis.

Bean picked something small and black out of his ear and flicked it away. "How many men have you got working on your farm?" he asked.

"Thirty-five," Boggis said.

"I've got thirty-six," Bunce said.

"And I've got thirty-seven," Bean said. "That makes one hundred and eight men altogether. We must order them to surround the hill. Each man will have a gun and a flashlight. There will be no escape then for Mr. Fox."

So the order went down to the farms, and that night one hundred and eight men formed a tight ring around the bottom of the hill. They were armed with sticks and guns and hatchets and pistols and all sorts of other horrible weapons. This made it quite impossible for a fox or indeed for any other animal to escape from the hill.

The next day, the watching and waiting went on. Boggis and Bunce and Bean sat upon small stools, staring at the fox's hole. They didn't talk much. They just sat there with their guns on their laps.

Every so often, Mr. Fox would creep a little closer toward the mouth of the tunnel and take a sniff. Then he would creep back again and say, "They're still there."

"Are you quite sure?" Mrs. Fox would ask.

"Positive," said Mr. Fox. "I can smell that man Bean a mile away. He stinks."

9

MR. FOX HAS A PLAN

For three days and three nights this waiting game went on.

"How long can a fox go without food or water?" Boggis asked on the third day.

"Not much longer now," Bean told him. "He'll make a run for it soon. He'll have to."

Bean was right. Down in the tunnel the foxes were slowly but surely starving to death.

"If only we could have just a tiny sip of water," said one of the Small Foxes. "Oh, Dad, can't you do *something*?"

"Couldn't we make a dash for it, Dad? We'd have a little bit of a chance, wouldn't we?"

"No chance at all," snapped Mrs. Fox. "I refuse to let you go up there and face those guns. I'd sooner you stay down here and die in peace."

Mr. Fox had not spoken for a long time. He had been sitting quite still, his eyes closed, not even hearing what the others were saying. Mrs. Fox knew that he was trying desperately to think of a way out. And now, as she looked at him, she saw him stir himself and get slowly to his feet. He looked back at his wife. There was a little spark of excitement dancing in his eyes.

"What it is, darling?" said Mrs. Fox quickly.

"I've just had a bit of an idea," Mr. Fox said carefully.

"What?" they cried. "Oh Dad, what is it?"

"Come *on!*" said Mrs. Fox. "Tell us quickly!"

"Well . . . " said Mr. Fox, then he stopped and sighed and sadly shook his head. He sat down again. "It's no good," he said. "It won't work after all."

"Why not, Dad?"

"Because it means more digging and we

35

aren't any of us strong enough for that after three days and nights without food."

"Yes we are, Dad!" cried the Small Foxes, jumping up and running to their father. "We can do it! You see if we can't! So can you!"

Mr. Fox looked at the four Small Foxes and he smiled. What fine children I have, he thought. They are starving to death and they haven't had a drink for three days, but they are still undefeated. I must not let them down.

"I . . . I suppose we could give it a try," he said.

"Let's go, Dad! Tell us what you want us to do!"

Slowly, Mrs. Fox got to her feet. She was suffering more than any of them from the lack of food and water. She was very weak. "I am so sorry," she said, "but I don't think I am going to be much help."

"You stay right where you are, my darling," said Mr. Fox. "We can handle this by ourselves."

10

BOGGIS'S CHICKEN-HOUSE
NUMBER ONE

"This time we must go in a very special direction," said Mr. Fox, pointing sideways and downward.

So he and his four children started to dig once again. The work went much more slowly now. Yet they kept at it with great courage, and little by little the tunnel began to grow.

"Dad, I wish you would tell us *where* we are going," said one of the children.

"I dare not do that," said Mr. Fox, "because this place I am *hoping* to get to is so *marvelous* that if I described it to you now you would go crazy with excitement. And then, if we failed to get there (which is very possible) you would die of disappointment. I don't want to raise your hopes too much, my darlings."

For a long long time they kept on digging. For how long they did not know, because there were no days and no nights down there in the murky tunnel. But at last Mr. Fox gave the order to stop. "I think," he said, "we had better take a peep upstairs now and see where we are. I know where I *want* to be, but I can't possibly be sure we're anywhere near it."

Slowly, wearily, the foxes began to slope the tunnel up toward the surface. Up and up it went . . . until suddenly they came to something hard above their heads and they couldn't go up any further. Mr. Fox reached up to examine this hard thing. "It's wood!" he whispered. "Wooden planks!"

"What does that mean, Dad?"

"It means, unless I am very much mistaken, that we are right underneath somebody's house," whispered Mr. Fox. "Be very quiet now while I take a peek."

Carefully, Mr. Fox began pushing up one of the floorboards. The board creaked most terribly and they all ducked down, waiting for something awful to happen. Nothing did. So Mr. Fox pushed up a second board. And then, very very cautiously, he poked his head up through the gap. He let out a shriek of excitement.

"I've done it!" he yelled. "I've done it *first time! I've done it! I've done it!"* He pulled himself up through the gap in the floor and started prancing and dancing with joy. "Come on up!" he sang out. "Come up and see where you are, my darlings! What a sight for a hungry fox! Hallelujah! Hooray! Hooray!"

The four Small Foxes scrambled up out of the tunnel and what a fantastic sight it was that now met their eyes! They were in a huge shed and the whole place was teeming with chickens. There were white chickens and brown chickens and black chickens by the thousand!

"Boggis's Chicken-House Number One!" cried Mr. Fox. "It's exactly what I was aiming at! I hit it slap in the middle! First time! Isn't that fantastic! *And,* if I may say so, rather clever!"

The Small Foxes went wild with excitement. They started running around in all directions, chasing the chickens.

"Wait!" ordered Mr. Fox. "Don't lose your heads! Stand back! Calm down! Let's do this

properly! First of all, everyone have a drink of water!"

They all ran over to the chickens' drinking-trough and lapped up the lovely cool water. Then Mr. Fox chose three of the plumpest hens, and with a clever flick of his jaws he killed them instantly.

"Back to the tunnel!" he ordered. "Come on! No fooling around! The quicker you move, the quicker you shall have something to eat!"

One after another, they climbed down through the hole in the floor and soon they were all standing once again in the dark tunnel. Mr. Fox reached up and pulled the floor-boards back into place. He did this with great care. He did it so that no one could tell they had ever been moved.

"My son," he said, giving the three plump hens to the biggest of his four small children, "run back with these to your mother. Tell her to prepare a feast. Tell her the rest of us will be along in a jiffy, as soon as we have made a few other little arrangements."

11

A SURPRISE FOR MRS. FOX

The Small Fox ran back along the tunnel as fast as he could, carrying the three plump hens. He was exploding with joy. "Just wait!" he kept thinking, "just wait till Mummy sees these!" He had a long way to run but he never stopped once on the way, and he came bursting in on Mrs. Fox. "Mummy!" he cried, out of breath. "Look Mummy, look! Wake up and see what I've brought you!"

Mrs. Fox, who was weaker than ever now from lack of food, opened one eye and looked at the hens. "I'm dreaming," she murmured and closed the eye again.

"You're not dreaming, Mummy! They're real chickens! We're saved! We're not going to starve!"

Mrs. Fox opened both eyes and sat up quickly. "But my *dear* child!" she cried. "Where on earth . . . ?"

"Boggis's Chicken-House Number One!" spluttered the Small Fox. "We tunnelled right up under the floor and you've never seen so

many big fat hens in all your life! And Dad said to prepare a feast! They'll be back soon!"

The sight of food seemed to give new strength to Mrs. Fox. "A feast it shall be!" she said, standing up. "Oh, what a fantastic fox your father is! Hurry up, child, and start plucking those chickens!"

Far away down in the tunnel, the fantastic Mr. Fox was saying, "Now for the next bit, my darlings! This one'll be as easy as pie! All we have to do is dig another little tunnel from *here* to there!"

"To where, Dad?"

"Don't ask so many questions. Start digging!"

12
BADGER

Mr. Fox and the three remaining Small Foxes dug fast and straight. They were all too excited now to feel tired or hungry. They knew they were going to have a whacking great feast before long and the fact that it was none other than Boggis's chickens they were going to eat made them chortle with laughter every time they thought of it. It was lovely to realize that while the fat farmer was sitting up there on the hill waiting for them to starve, he was also giving them their dinner without knowing it. "Keep digging," said Mr. Fox. "It's not much further."

All of a sudden a deep voice above their heads said, *"Who goes there?"* The foxes jumped. They looked up quickly and they saw, peeking through a small hole in the roof of the tunnel, a long black pointed furry face.

"Badger!" cried Mr. Fox.

"Foxy!" cried Badger. "My goodness me, I'm glad I've found *someone* at last! I've been digging around in circles for three days and nights and I haven't the foggiest idea where I am!"

Badger made the hole in the ceiling bigger and dropped down beside the foxes. A Small Badger (his son) dropped down after him. "Haven't you *heard* what's happening up on the hill?" Badger said excitedly. "It's chaos! Half the woods has disappeared and there are men with guns all over the countryside. None of us can get out, even at night! We're all starving to death!"

"Who is *we*?" asked Mr. Fox.

"All us diggers. That's me and Mole and

Rabbit and all our wives and children. Even Weasel, who can usually sneak out of the tightest spots, is right now hiding down my hole with Mrs. Weasel and six kids. What on earth are we going to do, Foxy? I think we're finished!"

Mr. Fox looked at his three children and he smiled. The children smiled back at him, sharing his secret. "My dear old Badger," he said, "this mess you're in is all my fault . . . "

"I *know* it's your fault!" said Badger furiously. "And the farmers are not going to give up till they've got you. Unfortunately, that means *us* as well. It means everyone on the hill." Badger sat down and put a paw around his small son. "We're done for," he said softly. "My poor wife up there is so weak she can't dig another yard."

"Nor can mine," said Mr. Fox. "And yet at this very minute she is preparing for me and my children the most delicious feast of plump juicy chickens . . . "

"Stop!" cried Badger. "Don't tease me! I can't stand it!"

"It's true!" cried the Small Foxes. "Dad's not teasing! We've got chickens galore!"

47

"And because everything is entirely my fault," said Mr. Fox, "I invite you to share the feast. I invite *everyone* to share it—you and Mole and Rabbit and Weasel and all your wives and children. There'll be plenty to go round, I can assure you."

"You mean it?" cried Badger. "You *really mean* it?"

Mr. Fox pushed his face close to Badger's and whispered darkly, *"Do you know* where we've just been?"

"Where?"

"Right inside Boggis's Chicken-House Number One!"

"No!"

"Yes! But that is nothing to where we are going now. You have come just at the right moment, my dear Badger. You can help us dig. And in the meanwhile, your small son can run back to Mrs. Badger and all the others and spread the good news." Mr. Fox turned to the Small Badger and said, "Tell them they are invited to a Fox's Feast. Then bring them all down here and follow this tunnel back until you find my home!"

"Yes, Mr. Fox!" said the Small Badger.

"Yes, sir! Right away, sir! Oh, thank you, sir!" and he scrambled quickly back through the hole in the roof of the tunnel and disappeared.

13

BUNCE'S GIANT STOREHOUSE

"My dear Foxy," cried Badger. "What in the world has happened to your tail?"

"Don't talk about it, *please*," said Mr. Fox. "It's a painful subject."

They were digging the new tunnel. They dug on in silence. Badger was a great digger and the tunnel went forward at a terrific pace now that he was lending a paw. Soon they were crouching underneath yet another wooden floor.

Mr. Fox grinned slyly, showing sharp white teeth. "If I am not mistaken, my dear Badger," he said, "we are now underneath the farm which belongs to that nasty little pot-bellied dwarf, Bunce. We are, in fact, directly underneath the most *interesting part* of that farm."

"Ducks and geese!" cried the Small Foxes, licking their lips. "Juicy tender ducks and big fat geese!"

"Ex-*actly!*" said Mr. Fox.

"But how in the world can you know where we are?" asked Badger.

Mr. Fox grinned again, showing even more white teeth. "Look," he said, "I know my way around these farms blindfolded. For me it's just as easy below ground as it is above it." He reached high and pushed up one wooden floorboard, then another. He poked his head through the gap.

"Yes!" he shouted, jumping up into the room above. "I've done it again! I've hit it smack on the nose! Right in the bull's-eye! Come and look!"

Quickly Badger and the three Small Foxes scrambled up after him. They stopped and stared. They stood and gaped. They were so overwhelmed they couldn't speak; for what they now saw was a kind of fox's dream, a badger's dream, a paradise for hungry animals.

"This, my dear old Badger," proclaimed Mr. Fox, "is Bunce's Mighty Storehouse! All

his finest stuff is stored in here before he sends it off to market."

Against all the four walls of the great room, stacked in cupboards and piled upon shelves reaching from floor to ceiling, were thousands and thousands of the finest and fattest ducks and geese, plucked and ready for roasting! And up above, dangling from the rafters, there must have been at least a hundred smoked hams and fifty sides of bacon!

"Just feast your eyes on *that!*" cried Mr. Fox, dancing up and down. "What d'you think of it, eh? Pretty good grub!"

Suddenly, as though springs had been released in their legs, the three hungry Small Foxes and the ravenously hungry Badger sprang forward to grab the luscious food.

"Stop!" ordered Mr. Fox. "This is *my* party, so *I* shall do the choosing." The others fell back, licking their chops. Mr. Fox began prowling around the storehouse examining the glorious display with an expert eye. A thread of saliva slid down one side of his jaw and hung suspended in midair, then snapped.

"We mustn't overdo it," he said. "Mustn't give the game away. Mustn't let them know what we've been up to. We must be neat and tidy and take just a few of the choicest morsels. So, to start with we shall have four plump young ducks." He took them from the shelf. "Oh, how lovely and fat they are! No wonder Bunce gets a special price for them in the market! . . . All right, Badger, lend me a hand to get them down . . . You children can help as well . . . There we go . . . Goodness me, look how your mouths are watering . . . And now . . . I think we had better have a few geese . . . Three will be quite enough . . . We'll take the biggest . . . Oh my, oh my, you'll never see finer geese than these in a king's kitchen . . . Gently does it . . . that's the way . . . And what about a couple of nice smoked hams . . . I adore smoked ham, don't you, Badger . . . Fetch me that stepladder, will you please . . ."

Mr. Fox climbed up the ladder and handed down three magnificent hams. "And do you like bacon, Badger?"

"I'm mad about bacon!" cried Badger, dancing with excitement. "Let's have a side of bacon! That big one up there!"

"And carrots, Dad!" said the smallest of the three Small Foxes. "We must take some of those carrots."

"Don't be a twerp," said Mr. Fox. "You know we never eat things like that."

"It's not for us, Dad. It's for the Rabbits. They only eat vegetables."

"My goodness me, you're right!" cried Mr. Fox. "What a thoughtful little fellow you are! Take ten bunches of carrots!"

Soon, all this lovely loot was lying in a neat heap upon the floor. The Small Foxes crouched close, their noses twitching, their eyes shining like stars.

"And now," said Mr. Fox, "we shall have to borrow from our friend Bunce two of those useful pushcarts over in the corner." He and Badger fetched the pushcarts, and the ducks and geese and hams and bacon were loaded on to them. Quickly the pushcarts were lowered through the hole in the floor. The animals slid down after them. Back in the tunnel, Mr. Fox again pulled the floorboards very carefully into place so that no one could see they had been moved.

"My darlings," he said, pointing to two of the three Small Foxes, "take a cart each and run back as fast as you can to your mother. Give her my love and tell her we are having guests for dinner—the Badgers, the Moles, the Rabbits and the Weasels. Tell her it must be a truly great feast. And tell her the rest of us will be home as soon as we've done one more little job."

"Yes, Dad! Right away, Dad!" they answered, and they grabbed a trolley each and went rushing off down the tunnel.

14

BADGER HAS DOUBTS

"Just one more visit!" cried Mr. Fox.

"And I'll bet I know where that'll be," said the only Small Fox now left. He was the Smallest Fox of them all.

"Where?" asked Badger.

"Well," said the Smallest Fox. "We've been to Boggis and we've been to Bunce but we haven't been to Bean. It must be Bean."

"You are right," said Mr. Fox. "But what you don't know is which *part* of Bean's place we are about to visit."

"Which?" they said both together.

"Ah-ha," said Mr. Fox. "Just you wait and see." They were digging as they talked. The tunnel was going forward fast.

Suddenly Badger said, "Doesn't this worry you just a tiny bit, Foxy?"

"Worry me?" said Mr. Fox. "What?"

"All this . . . this *stealing*."

Mr. Fox stopped digging and stared at Badger as though he had gone completely dotty. "My dear old furry frump," he said, "do you know anyone in the *whole world* who wouldn't swipe a few chickens if their children were starving to death?"

There was a short silence while Badger thought deeply about this.

"You are far too respectable," said Mr. Fox.

"There's nothing wrong with being respectable," Badger said.

"Look," said Mr. Fox. "Boggis and Bunce

and Bean are out to *kill* us, you realize that, I hope?"

"I do, Foxy, I do indeed," said the gentle Badger.

"But *we're* not going to stoop to *their* level. We don't want to kill *them.*"

"I should hope not indeed," said Mr. Badger.

"We wouldn't dream of it," said Mr. Fox. "We shall simply take a little food here and there to keep us and our families alive. Right?"

"I suppose we'll have to," said Badger.

"If *they* want to be horrible, let them," said Mr. Fox. "We down here are decent peace-loving creatures."

Badger laid his head on one side and smiled at Mr. Fox. "Foxy," he said, "I love you."

"Thank you," said Mr. Fox. "And now let's get on with the digging."

Five minutes later, Badger's front paws hit against something flat and hard. "What on earth is this?" he said. "It looks like a solid stone wall." He and Mr. Fox scraped away the soil. It *was* a wall. But it was built of bricks not stones. The wall was right in front of them, blocking their way.

"Now who in the world would build a wall under the ground?" asked Badger.

"Very simple," said Mr. Fox. "It's the wall of an underground room. And if I am not mistaken, it is exactly what I'm looking for."

15

BEAN'S SECRET CIDER CELLAR

Mr. Fox examined the wall carefully. He saw that the cement between the bricks was old and crumbly, so he loosened a brick without much trouble and pulled it away. Suddenly, out from the hole where the brick had been, there popped a small sharp face with whiskers. "Go away!" it snapped. "You can't come in here! It's private!"

"Good Lord!" said Badger. "It's Rat!"

"You saucy beast!" said Mr. Fox. "I should have guessed we'd find you down here somewhere."

"Go away!" shrieked Rat. "Go on, beat it! This is my private pitch!"

"Shut up," said Mr. Fox.

"I will not shut up!" shrieked Rat. "This is *my* place! I got here first!"

Mr. Fox gave a brilliant smile, flashing his white teeth. "My dear Rat," he said softly, "I am a hungry fellow and if you don't hop it quickly I shall eat-you-up-in-one-gulp!"

That did it. Rat popped back fast out of sight. Mr. Fox laughed and began pulling more bricks out of the wall. When he had made a biggish hole, he crept through it. Badger and the Smallest Fox followed him in.

They found themselves in a vast, damp, gloomy cellar. "This is it!" cried Mr. Fox.

"This is *what?*" said Badger. "The place is empty."

"Where are the turkeys?" asked the Smallest Fox, staring into the gloom. "I thought Bean was a turkey man."

"He is a turkey man," said Mr. Fox. "But

we're not after turkeys now. We've got plenty of food."

"Then what *do* we need, Dad?"

"Take a good look round," said Mr. Fox. "Don't you see *anything* that interests you?"

Badger and the Smallest Fox peered into the half-darkness. As their eyes became accustomed to the gloom, they began to see what looked like a whole lot of big glass jars standing upon shelves around the walls. They went closer. They *were* jars. There were hundreds of them, and upon each one was written the word CIDER.

The Smallest Fox leaped high in the air. "Oh Dad!" he cried out. "Look what we've found! It's cider!"

"Ex-*actly*," said Mr. Fox.

"Tremendous!" shouted Badger.

"Bean's Secret Cider Cellar," said Mr. Fox. "But go carefully, my dears. Don't make a noise. This cellar is right underneath the farmhouse itself."

"Cider," said Badger, "is especially good for Badgers. We take it as medicine—one large glassful three times a day with meals and another at bedtime."

"It will make the feast into a banquet," said Mr. Fox.

While they were talking, the Smallest Fox had sneaked a jar off the shelf and had taken a gulp. "Wow!" he gasped. "Wow-*ee!*"

You must understand this was not the ordinary weak fizzy cider one buys in a store. It was the real stuff, a home-brewed fiery liquor that burned in your throat and boiled in your stomach.

"Ah-h-h-h-h-h!" gasped the Smallest Fox. "This is *some cider!*"

"That's quite enough of that," said Mr. Fox, grabbing the jar and putting it to his own lips. He took a tremendous gulp. "It's miraculous!" he whispered, fighting for breath. "It's fabulous! It's beautiful!"

"It's my turn," said Badger, taking the jar and tilting his head well back. The cider gurgled and bubbled down his throat. "It's . . . it's like melted gold!" he gasped. "Oh Foxy, it's . . . it's like drinking sunbeams and rainbows!"

"You're poaching!" shrieked Rat. "Put that down at once! There'll be none left for me!" Rat was perched upon the highest shelf in the cellar, peering out from behind a huge jar.

There was a small rubber tube inserted in the neck of the jar, and Rat was using this tube to suck out the cider.

"You're drunk!" said Mr. Fox.

"Mind your own business!" shrieked Rat. "And if you great clumsy brutes come messing about in here we'll all be caught! Get out and leave me to sip my cider in peace."

At that moment they heard a woman's voice calling out in the house above them. "Hurry up and get that cider, Mabel!" the voice called. "You know Mr. Bean doesn't like to be kept waiting! Especially when he's been out all night in a tent!"

The animals froze. They stayed absolutely still, their ears pricked, their bodies tense.

Then they heard the sound of a door being opened. The door was at the top of a flight of stone steps leading down from the house to the cellar.

And now someone was starting to come down those steps.

16

THE WOMAN

"Quick!" said Mr. Fox. "Hide!" He and Badger and the Smallest Fox jumped up onto a shelf and crouched behind a row of big cider jars. Peering around the jars, they saw a huge woman coming down into the cellar. At the foot of the steps, the woman paused, looking right and left. Then she turned and headed straight for the place where Mr. Fox and Badger and the Smallest Fox were hiding. She stopped right in front of them. The only thing between her and them was a row of cider jars. She was so close, Mr. Fox could hear the sound of her breathing. Peeping through the crack between two bottles, he noticed that she carried a big rolling pin in one hand.

"How many will he want this time, Mrs. Bean?" the woman shouted. And from the top of the steps the other voice called back. "Bring up two or three jars."

"He drank four yesterday, Mrs. Bean."

"Yes, but he won't want that many today because he's not going to be up there more than a few hours longer. He says the fox is bound to make a run for it this morning. It can't possibly stay down that hole another day without food."

The woman in the cellar reached out and lifted a jar of cider from the shelf. The jar she took was next but one to the jar behind which Mr. Fox was crouching.

"I'll be glad when the rotten brute is killed and strung up on the front porch," she called out. "And by the way, Mrs. Bean, your hus-band promised I could have the tail as a souvenir."

"The tail's been all shot to pieces," said the voice from upstairs. "Didn't you know that?"

"You mean it's *ruined?*"

"Of course, it's ruined. They shot the tail but missed the fox."

"Oh heck!" said the big woman. "I did so want that tail!"

"You can have the head instead, Mabel. You can get it stuffed and hang it on your bedroom wall. Hurry up now with that cider!"

"Yes, ma'am, I'm coming," said the big woman, and she took a second jar from the shelf.

If she takes one more, she'll see us, thought Mr. Fox. He could feel the Smallest Fox's body pressed tightly against his own, quivering with excitement.

"Will two be enough, Mrs. Bean, or shall I take three?"

"My goodness, Mabel, I don't care so long as you get a move on!"

"Then two it is," said the huge woman, speaking to herself now. "He drinks too much anyway."

Carrying a jar in each hand and with the rolling pin tucked under one arm, she walked away across the cellar. At the foot of the steps she paused and looked around, sniffing the air. "There's rats down here again, Mrs. Bean. I can smell 'em."

"Then poison them, woman, poison them! You know where the poison's kept."

"Yes, ma'am," Mabel said. She climbed slowly out of sight up the steps. The door slammed.

"Quick!" said Mr. Fox. "Grab a jar each and run for it!"

Rat stood on his high shelf and shrieked, "What did I tell you! You nearly got nabbed, didn't you? You nearly gave the game away! You keep out of here from now on! I don't want you around! This is my place!"

"*You,*" said Mr. Fox, "are you going to be poisoned."

"Poppycock!" said Rat. "I sit up here and watch her putting the stuff down. She'll never get *me.*"

Mr. Fox and Badger and the Smallest Fox ran across the cellar clutching a gallon jar each. "Good-bye Rat!" they called out as they disappeared through the hole in the wall. "Thanks for the lovely cider!"

"Thieves!" shrieked Rat. "Robbers! Bandits! Burglars!"

17

THE GREAT FEAST

Back in the tunnel they paused so that Mr. Fox could brick up the hole in the wall. He was humming to himself as he put the bricks back in place. "I can still taste that glorious cider," he said. "What an impudent fellow Rat is."

"He has bad manners," Badger said. "All rats have bad manners. I've never met a polite rat yet."

"And he drinks too much," said Mr. Fox, putting the last brick in place. "There we are. Now, home to the feast!"

They grabbed their jars of cider and off they went. Mr. Fox was in front, the Smallest Fox came next and Badger last. Along the tunnel they flew . . . past the turning that led to Bunce's Mighty Storehouse . . . past Boggis's Chicken-House Number One, and then up the long home stretch toward the place where they knew Mrs. Fox would be waiting.

"Keep it up, my darlings!" shouted Mr. Fox. "We'll soon be there! Think what's waiting for us at the other end! And just think what we're bringing home with us in these jars! That ought to cheer up poor Mrs. Fox." Mr. Fox sang a little song as he ran:

"Home again swiftly I glide,
Back to my beautiful bride.
She'll not feel so rotten
As soon as she's gotten
Some cider inside her inside."

Then Badger joined in:

"Oh poor Mrs. Badger," he cried,
"So hungry she very near died.
But she'll not feel so hollow
If only she'll swallow
Some cider inside her inside."

They were still singing as they rounded the final corner and burst in upon the most wonderful and amazing sight any of them had ever seen. The feast was just beginning. A large dining room had been hollowed out of the earth, and in the middle of it, seated around a huge table, were no less than twenty-nine animals. They were:

Mrs. Fox and Three Small Foxes.

Mrs. Badger and Three Small Badgers.

Mole and Mrs. Mole and four Small Moles.

Rabbit and Mrs. Rabbit and five small Rabbits.

Weasel and Mrs. Weasel and six Small Weasels.

The table was covered with chickens and ducks and geese and hams and bacon, and everyone was tucking in to the lovely food.

"My darling!" cried Mrs. Fox, jumping up

and hugging Mr. Fox. "We couldn't wait! Please forgive us!" Then she hugged the Smallest Fox of all, and Mrs. Badger hugged Badger, and everyone hugged everyone else. Amid shouts of joy, the great jars of cider were placed upon the table, and Mr. Fox and Badger and the Smallest Fox sat down with the others.

You must remember no one had eaten a thing for several days. They were ravenous. So for a while there was no conversation at all. There was only the sound of crunching and chewing as the animals attacked the succulent food.

At last, Badger stood up. He raised his glass of cider and called out, "A toast! I want you all to stand and drink a toast to our dear friend who has saved our lives this day—Mr. Fox!"

"To Mr. Fox!" They all shouted, standing up and raising their glasses. "To Mr. Fox! Long may he live!"

Then Mrs. Fox got shyly to her feet and said, "I don't want to make a speech. I just want to say one thing, and it is this: MY HUS-BAND IS A FANTASTIC FOX." Everyone clapped and cheered. Then Mr. Fox himself stood up.

"This delicious meal . . . ," he began, then he stopped. In the silence that followed, he let fly a tremendous belch. There was laughter and more clapping. "This delicious meal, my friends," he went on, "is by courtesy of Messrs. Boggis, Bunce and Bean." (More cheering and laughter.) "And I hope you have enjoyed it as much as I have." He let fly another colossal belch.

"Better out than in," said Badger.

"Thank you," said Mr. Fox, grinning hugely. "But now, my friends, let us be serious. Let us think of tomorrow and the next day and the days after that. If we go out, we will be killed. Right?"

"Right!" they shouted.

"We'll be shot before we've gone a yard," said Badger.

"Ex-*actly*," said Mr. Fox, "But who *wants* to go out, anyway, let me ask you that? We are all diggers, every one of us. We hate the outside. The outside is full of enemies. We only go out because we have to, to get food for our families. But now, my friends, we have an entirely new set-up. We have a safe tunnel leading to three of the finest stores in the world!"

"We do indeed!" said Badger. "I've seen 'em!"

"And you know what this means?" said Mr. Fox. "*It means that none of us need ever go out into the open again!*"

There was a buzz of excitement around the table.

"I therefore invite you all," Mr. Fox went on, "to stay here with me forever."

"Forever!" they cried. "My goodness! How

marvelous!" And Rabbit said to Mrs. Rabbit, "My dear, just think! We're never going to be shot at again in our lives!"

"We will make," said Mr. Fox, "a little underground village, with streets and houses on each side—separate houses for Badgers and Moles and Rabbits and Weasels and Foxes. And every day I will go shopping for you all. And every day we will eat like kings."

The cheering that followed this speech went on for many minutes.

18

STILL WAITING

Outside the fox's hole, Boggis and Bunce and Bean sat beside their tents with their guns on their laps. It was beginning to rain. Water was trickling down the necks of the three men and into their shoes.

"He won't stay down there much longer now," Boggis said.

"The brute must be famished," Bunce said.

"That's right," Bean said. "He'll be making a dash for it any moment. Keep your guns handy."

They sat there by the hole, waiting for the fox to come out.

And so far as I know, they are still waiting.

ABOUT THE AUTHOR

ROALD DAHL's books for children include *James and the Giant Peach, Charlie and the Great Glass Elevator, Danny The Champion of the World, Fantastic Mr. Fox* and of course the great and glorious, *Charlie and the Chocolate Factory.* Mr. Dahl lives with his wife Academy Award-winning actress Patricia Neal and their four children in the village of Great Missenden, Buckinghamshire, England.

FROM THE SPOOKY, EERIE PEN OF JOHN BELLAIRS . . .

☐ **THE CURSE OF THE**   15540/$2.95
   BLUE FIGURINE

Johnny Dixon knows a lot about ancient Egypt and curses and evil spirits—but when he finds the blue figurine, he actually "sees" a frightening, super-natural world. Even his friend Professor Childermass can't help him!

☐ **THE MUMMY, THE WILL**   15498/$2.75
   AND THE CRYPT

For months Johnny has been working on a riddle that would lead to a $10,000 reward. Feeling certain that the money is hidden somewhere in the house of a dead man, Johnny goes into his house where a bolt of lightning reveals to him that the house is not quite deserted . . .

☐ **THE SPELL OF THE**   15357/$2.50
   SORCERER'S SKULL

Johnny Dixon is back, but this time he's not teamed up with Dr. Childermass. That's because his friend, the Professor, has disappeared!

Shop at home
for quality children's books
and save money, too.

Now you can order books for the whole family from Bantam's latest catalog of hundreds of titles including many fine children's books. *And* this special offer gives you an opportunity to purchase a Bantam book for only 50¢. Here's how:

By ordering any five books at the regular price per order, you can also choose any other single book listed (up to a $5.95 value) for just 50¢. Some restrictions do apply, so for further details send for Bantam's catalog of titles today.